This edition published in 1990 by Gallery Books,
an imprint of W.H. Smith Publishers, Inc.
112 Madison Avenue, New York, New York 10016

Produced for Gallery Books by Joshua Morris Publishing, Inc.,
221 Danbury Road, Wilton, CT 06897

Gallery Books are available for bulk purchase
for sales promotions and premium use.
For details write or telephone the Manager of Special Sales,
W.H. Smith Publishers, Inc., 112 Madison Avenue,
New York, New York 10016   (212) 532-6600.

The Velveteen Rabbit

Illustrated by Loretta Krupinski

GALLERY BOOKS
An Imprint of W. H. Smith Publishers Inc.
112 Madison Avenue
New York City 10016

There once was a Velveteen Rabbit, as fat and splendid as a rabbit should be. It was tucked into a little Boy's stocking on Christmas morning.

There were other toys in the stocking,
but the Rabbit was by far the best.
The Boy played with him for a
few hours. But then the Aunts
and Uncles came with more
presents. In the excitement,
the Rabbit was forgotten.

For a long while, the Rabbit lived in the Boy's room, where his only friend was the wise old Toy Horse. One day, the Toy Horse told him that sometimes a toy could become Real.

"What is Real?" asked the Rabbit.
"When a child loves you, REALLY loves you," said the Toy Horse "then you become Real."
The Rabbit sighed. He wanted to be Real, too.

Then, one night, the little Boy took the Rabbit to bed with him. And every night after that, the Boy refused to go to bed without the Rabbit. The Boy hugged him tight and kissed him on the nose before going to sleep.

One night the nurse Nana had to go outside in
the dark to find the Rabbit. She said, "I've never
seen such a fuss over a toy!"

"He isn't a toy. He's Real!" the Boy cried.
When the Rabbit heard that, he thought his heart
would burst for joy.

That was a wonderful summer. Each long
afternoon, the Boy and the Rabbit would play in
the garden.

One day, the Rabbit saw two strange creatures.
They were rabbits like himself, but they were very
well made.

"Can you hop?" one of them asked.

"He can't," said the other. "He isn't Real!"

"I am Real!" the Rabbit shouted. "The Boy said so!"

But the two wild rabbits just ran away.

Then, one morning, the Boy was very sick.
For a while, it seemed that he wouldn't get well.
But, after many days, his fever went away. He was
going to get better!

The doctor ordered that the room be cleaned
and that all the toys in the room be burned.

"But how about his old bunny?" asked Nana.

"It's full of germs," said the doctor. "Burn it
at once."

So the Velveteen Rabbit was put into a bag and carried out to the backyard. How lonely he felt! He thought of all those happy hours he had played with the Boy. Suddenly a big, wet tear trickled down his nose and fell to the ground.

Where the tear had fallen, a wonderful flower
grew! Out of its petals stepped a beautiful fairy.
"Little Rabbit," she said, "come with me, and
I shall make you Real."

"Wasn't I Real before?" asked the Rabbit.

"You were Real to the Boy because he loved you. Now you will be Real to *everyone*," said the fairy.

Then she kissed him.

Then the Velveteen Rabbit did something he had never done before. He hopped! And he hopped again—just like all the other rabbits. The fairy's kiss had made him really REAL!

The next spring, the Boy saw two small rabbits in the garden. One was brown all over, but the other looked different somehow.

"Why, he looks just like my old Bunny who was lost when I was sick!" said the Boy.

And it really was his old Bunny. The Bunny had come back to look at the child who first loved him and helped him to be Real.